I0684818

Empty Tomb, Full Hearts

A Selection of Testimonies Among Those Who Saw the Risen Christ

Imagined by
James J. Stewart

*After his suffering, he [Jesus]
presented himself to them and gave
many convincing proofs that he
was alive. He appeared to them
over a period of forty days and
spoke about the kingdom of God.*
[Acts 1:3 (NIV2011)]

Preface

This is historical fiction based upon information found in the Bible, coupled with a variety of traditions. Many of the people portrayed here are identified as saints in Roman Catholic, Eastern Orthodox, Oriental Orthodox, and Coptic traditions. One of the definitions of Merriam-Webster describes *tradition* as "a belief or story or a body of beliefs or stories relating to the past that are commonly accepted as historical though not verifiable." This book reflects upon those traditions, woven together with Biblical passages.

When the testimonies in this book quote material found in the Bible, it is in italics, to separate clearly the biblical records from the traditional material or material from the author's imagination. Anyone who is interested in more details regarding the traditions surrounding the people portrayed throughout this book can find further information in public libraries or on the Internet.

The Apostle Paul offers us his own list of people who saw Jesus after his resurrection.

> *For I delivered to you as of first importance what I also received: that Christ died for our sins in accordance with the Scriptures, that he was buried, that he was raised on the third day in accordance with the Scriptures, and that <u>he appeared to Cephas</u>, then <u>to the twelve</u>. Then he appeared <u>to more than five hundred brothers at one time,</u> most of whom are still*

alive, though some have fallen asleep. Then he appeared <u>to James</u>, then <u>to all the apostles</u>. Last of all, as to one untimely born, he appeared also <u>to me</u>. For I am the least of the apostles, unworthy to be called an apostle, because I persecuted the church of God. (The underlining is mine.)

[1 Corinthians 15:3-9 (ESV)]

This book began with making a list of people who come to mind when we consider possible witnesses to the resurrection of Jesus Christ. The list is not alphabetized, though the table of contents that follows has been alphabetized to provide a quick index. The order of the testimonies is not based upon chronology or importance.

List of Testimonies

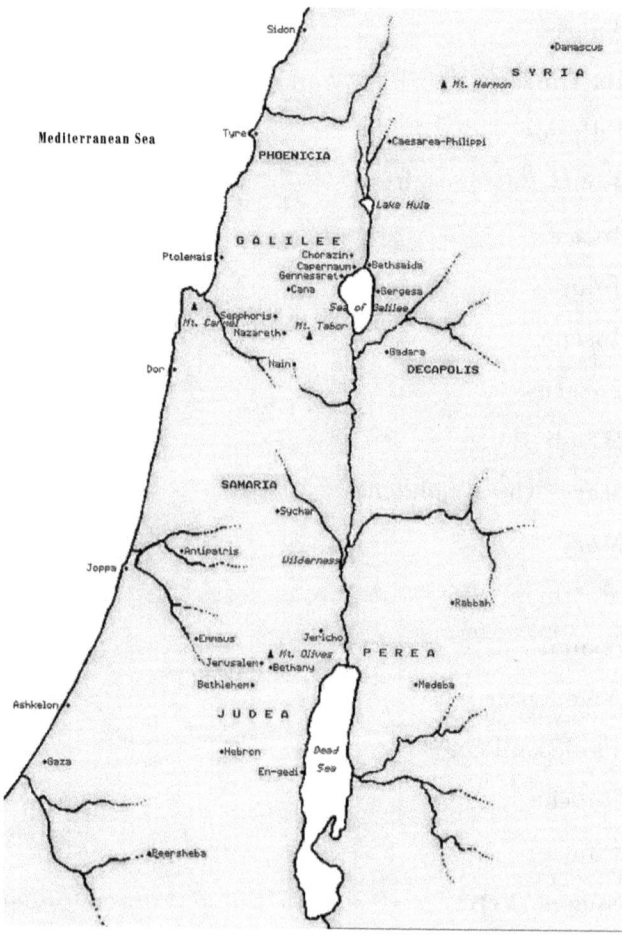

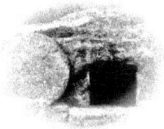

The Testimony of
Lazarus

> Lazarus was a friend of Jesus who sheltered
> and fed the Messiah on his trips to Jerusalem.

I know what it is like to walk out of a tomb and leave it empty. I did it, but it was not my doing.

Most of my life I was healthy. Like most people during my time, I worked long days, out in the blazing sun. When I got sick, at the first I thought I was just tired. My servants took up the slack for the work that had to be done to stay in business.

Then things got worse. My sisters did their best to take care of me. "You've got to eat, Lazarus," said my sister Martha countless times. She was a good cook, but nothing appealed to me.

While keeping me well fed, they told me they had sent for our Lord and friend, Jesus, who they wanted to pray for me. I was feeling horrible that night when I went to sleep.

The next thing I knew, I awakened in darkness. I heard my friend Jesus's voice calling me, saying, *"Come out!"* [John 11:43 (ESV)]

I made my way through the darkness towards the voice I heard. Then, people were pulling bandages off me. As the strips of cloth were removed from my face, I saw my friend Jesus standing there with my sisters, and they were all smiling. We embraced, and I felt great! There was a crowd of other people gathered around us. I knew most of them, but even the few strangers that I saw were as excited as I was.

I don't remember very much of the remainder of that day. Dozens of people joined my friend, my sisters, and I, as we ate and drank and enjoyed each other's company. It was long after sunset when I went to bed.

The Feast of Unleavened Bread was beginning, so Jesus and his closest circle of friends went on towards Jerusalem while I lingered in Bethany. I planned on joining them for a Feast of Unleavened Bread meal later in the week. That never happened. On the eve of that following Sabbath, my Lord and friend was executed. The ruling council of Jewish judges who govern all of Israel within the Roman Empire is called the Sanhedrin, and they condemned Jesus.

What I saw that Sabbath's eve will be forever burned into my memory. Mary, Martha, and I wept as we stood there. We were helpless to do anything but watch. The soldiers nailed a sign above his head, "The King of the Jews." It was in our native Hebrew, but it was repeated in Latin and in Greek. Other nails were put in Our Lord, so he would hang upon the cross from his hands and feet.

We could not leave him. All we could do was wait. Jesus gave up his spirit in the middle of the afternoon.

> *Since it was the day of Preparation, and so*
> *that the bodies would not remain on the cross*
> *on the Sabbath (for that Sabbath was a high*
> *day), the Jews asked Pilate that their legs*
> *might be broken and that they might be taken*
> *away. So the soldiers came and broke the legs*
> *of the first, and of the other who had been*
> *crucified with him. But when they came to*
> *Jesus and saw that he was already dead, they*
> *did not break his legs. But one of the soldiers*
> *pierced his side with a spear, and at once*
> *there came out blood and water.*
>
> [John 19:31-34 (ESV)

Not long after, a member of the Sanhedrin named Joseph took away his body. My sisters and I went home, walking back to Bethany out of habit, but we hardly knew where we were, or where we were going. The next day was a sad Sabbath.

After the Sabbath's sun went down, my sisters gathered some of the same kinds of spices they had used to bury me a week earlier. They left during the night because they wanted to be at the tomb when the sun rose. Jesus' body had been wrapped in a simple shroud when he was put in Joseph's tomb. My sisters wanted to give him a more proper burial with the spices. Another woman was to meet them there and help them.

Once again, it was not to be. The tomb was empty. I love saying that! It's true! The tomb was empty! The tomb was empty! An angel told my sisters and their friend that Jesus would meet his followers in Galilee.

When my sisters told me, I thought about it carefully. "Yes!" I told them. "The Zebedee family has a fishing business in Bethsaida. The ministry base of our Lord was in a town on the western shore of the Sea of Galilee, just west of Bethsaida. It is called Capernaum."

Mary nodded. "Yes! I remember! Let's go there."

Martha also nodded. "We must put together provisions for our journey," she said.

I told our servants where we were going and gave them instructions. After breaking bread at mid-day and satisfying our thirsts, we began our journey north.

Over the next several weeks, we journeyed around the Tiberias Sea area. Jesus appeared several times. We ate with him, drank with him, and conversed with him. We encountered hundreds of men, as well as women, children, and servants who often joined us.

I heard that the temple leaders wanted me executed because of my friendship with Jesus, and because He raised me from the dead. I was warned by several people that my sisters and I should not return to Judea. We prayed about it, and I decided that we should not abandon our ancestral home. We did not return directly south along the Jordan River, the way we had come. I decided to visit my cousins in Caesarea, on the coast. We traveled there by way of Nazareth and Megiddo. My sisters and I enjoyed visiting our cousins for two weeks. We shared the good news with them and relaxed on the Mediterranean.

Thus, it was more than two months before we returned home with full hearts. God had watched over our land and our servants while we were away. We journeyed to the Temple for Rosh Hashanah, but we were in no danger. We were told by other believers that the Sanhedrin did not want to stir up the past by arresting me. Our hearts remained full.

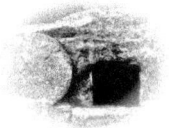

The Testimony of
"Naomi"

"Naomi" had menstrual bleeding for years when, in faith, she touched Jesus' clothing and was healed.

My testimony begins more than a year before that of Lazarus. I'm sure my Lord Jesus knew my name, but to His close friends traveling with him, I was simply a face among the crowd.

I was one very lonely woman. For twelve years, my menstruating did not stop. Since I was ceremonially unclean because of my bleeding, I could not approach anyone in my family. Cleanliness, law, and tradition are important. I could not eat with anyone, and I had to sleep by myself. My husband loved me and was very understanding.

I had heard of Jesus and knew he was going to pass through my community. I wanted to see him. I thought that, if I could just get close enough, perhaps close enough to touch even the bottom hem of his robe, that conceivably I could be healed. As I worked my way though the crowd, I had to keep myself mostly covered, including my face. I did not want to be recognized.

Jesus' robe barely touched the tips of my fingers when I felt warmth flow over me and through me.

> *And Jesus, perceiving in himself that power*
> *had gone out from him, immediately turned*
> *about in the crowd and said, "Who touched*
> *my garments?" And his disciples said to him,*
> *"You see the crowd pressing around you, and*
> *yet you say, 'Who touched me?'" And he*
> *looked around to see who had done it. But the*
> *woman, knowing what had happened to her,*
> *came in fear and trembling and fell down*
> *before him and told him the whole truth.*
> [Mark 5:30-33 (ESV)]

I was speechless at first. I knew that I had
been healed. The words suddenly gushed out of
me, and I explained everything. Jesus was so kind
in his response.

> *And he said to her, "Daughter, your faith*
> *has made you well; go in peace, and be*
> *healed of your disease." [Mark 5:34 (ESV)]*

He smiled at me, and the others smiled at me too.
The crowd stood with me, motionless, as Jesus and
his followers moved on. More than a year passed,
but I continued to hear stories about my Lord.

I did not see Jesus again until after my family
and I heard that Jesus had been executed. Then,
I heard he was alive and appearing in places near
to me. I was making some purchases in Bethsaida,
and a very large and imposing man approached
me. "You are the woman who was healed from her
bleeding. How are you"? he asked.

"I am well, sir," I said.

"I am called Peter. You and your family are
welcome to join us this evening by the Sea. I will
broil some fish."

"Will Our Lord be there?"

He smiled. "We can hope so. Through his resurrection from the dead, we have an imperishable, undefiled, and unfading inheritance that is kept in heaven for all of us who follow him."

"After my bleeding stopped, and after my Rabbi certified that I was no longer ceremonially unclean, my whole family was healed. My husband and I will be there." I felt excitement within me.

That evening, there were more than twenty of us there, and Jesus patiently taught us and answered our questions well into the night. Our hearts were filled as we listened to his voice. Listening to Jesus, I felt warm and at peace.

During my lifetime, I listened to many rabbis, both in the temple and at home. Jesus spoke as one with authority rather than quoting sources. It was as though we were listening to God. Since Jesus is God's son, that makes sense.

After Jesus disappeared, my family had only a few hours before the sun rose upon another day of work. Our hearts remained full.

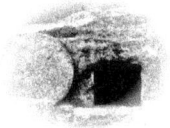

The Testimony of
Bartimaeus

Bartimaeus regained his sight less than a
week before Jesus was crucified.

I was born in Jericho, and I was blind. My
family has had land near Jericho ever since Moses
ascended to heaven, and Joshua entered and
conquered the land that had been promised by
God to his people. In my youth, my father,
Timaeus, always made sure my needs were being
met. Despite my blindness, he arranged for me to
be married. My wife and I raised a family. We got
by. Almighty God watched over us.

One spring, I was sitting under a tree beside
the main road leading to Jerusalem. For more
than two years I had been hearing stories about
Jesus, his teachings, and miracles. That day, I
heard someone mention that they saw Jesus
coming. I had heard of him.

When I was younger, my wife and I went to
be baptized by John the Baptist. That same day I
listened, as John had baptized Jesus. My wife told
me she saw a dove suddenly appear, and I heard
an amazingly deep voice from above say, *"This is
my beloved son, in whom I am well pleased."* I set
that into my mind: Jesus is God's beloved son.

So, it was on a day when I was sitting under
a tree, that I listened carefully to everything that

was happening. When I could tell that Jesus was
close, I called out as loud as I could:

> *"Jesus, Son of David, have mercy on me!"*
> *And many rebuked him, telling him to be*
> *silent. But he cried out all the more, "Son of*
> *David, have mercy on me!"*
> [Mark 10:47b-48 (ESV)]

I kept calling out because I could sense that
Jesus had not moved on. I heard him tell his
disciples to call me, and someone came closer to
me and told me to get up, which I did quickly. As
I came to him, he spoke to me.

> *And Jesus said to him, "What do you want*
> *me to do for you?" And the blind man said to*
> *him, "Rabbi, let me recover my sight." And*
> *Jesus said to him, "Go your way; your faith*
> *has made you well."*
> [Mark 10:51-52a (ESV)]

Suddenly, I could see! I could see! I was looking
directly at Jesus' face! There was no way I could
go home! I followed him.

My heart was full of wonder as we climbed up
the steep hill towards Jerusalem. My family had
taken me to Jerusalem previously, but for the first
time I saw with my own eyes the rugged terrain. I
also studied the faces of everyone who walked
with us. I was actually seeing the world with new
eyes. I experienced it differently!

I heard someone panting, and I looked back
to see a woman struggling to reach me.
"Bartimaeus!" My mouth dropped open, and I
was filled with joy because it was the voice of my

beloved wife, Orpah. "Matthew told me Jesus had healed you, and I had to be with you!" she said.

For the first time I was seeing her beautiful face, and we embraced. My love for Orpah was renewed and magnified! Both our hearts were full. We continued to climb towards Bethany, where we spent the Sabbath. A wonderful family led by a man named Lazarus fed us generously in their home. Lazarus said he cared for us because we were traveling with his friend and Lord, Jesus.

The first day of the week, as we moved towards Jerusalem, crowds began to surround us. Jesus got onto a donkey, and as he rode towards the gate, the people surrounding us began to respond:

> *And they brought the colt to Jesus and threw their cloaks on it, and he sat on it. And many spread their cloaks on the road, and others spread leafy branches that they had cut from the fields. And those who went before and those who followed were shouting, "Hosanna! Blessed is he who comes in the name of the Lord! Blessed is the coming kingdom of our father David! Hosanna in the highest!"*
> [Mark 11:7-10 (ESV)]

This continued until he entered the temple. Through most of that week, we saw Jesus and his disciples from time to time in the temple. It was Passover, and throughout each day the aromas of roasting meat filled the air.

On the day before the Sabbath, my wife and I awakened to great confusion. We learned that Rome was going to execute three criminals just outside the city. We did not want to see it, so we walked towards the temple. As we were doing so, we learned that one of the three men was Jesus.

Orpah and I were dumbfounded. Jesus? We made our way back to Bethany that day Jesus was crucified. For the rest of that day and into the Sabbath, we were in a haze of confusion. Jesus was Messiah! Why was he killed?

We remained in Bethany when Lazarus' sisters, Martha and Mary, went to the tomb to embalm Jesus. Midway through the morning, the two women came walking rapidly up the hill towards the house of Lazarus and his family. Jesus was alive!

Once again, our hearts were filled. Orpah and I returned to Jericho, elated. We decided along the way that we would talk to our servants, and then we would follow the Jordan River northward up to Galilee. We hoped to see Jesus again there, as he had promised his disciples.

Orpah and I saw Jesus several times over the next month before he returned to heaven. Though we no longer see him, we know he is with us. Our hearts are always full.

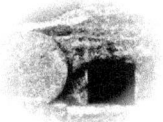

The Testimony of
Mary

> The mother of Jesus knew Him better than anyone and was present at His crucifixion.

I grew up in a typical Jewish household in Nazareth. My mother taught me all the things a girl should know. When I began to grow towards being a woman, my Father was approached by a man named Joseph in the market. Joseph had lost his wife while she gave birth, and he understood that my father had a daughter who was not spoken for. They came to an agreement. As soon as I showed signs of being ready to bear children, the wedding would take place. From that time on, I looked forward to living the simple life of a carpenter's wife, and being the mother to his children.

God had other plans, however. Everyone who knows me knows what happened. My life's plans were interrupted by a visit from an angel. Joseph and I became the parents of my first child, who was conceived when the Holy Spirit came upon me. The angel said to name him Jesus, and that he was to be called *Emmanuel*, which means "God with us."

That interruption of our lives became a divine intervention for everyone everywhere from that time forward. Joseph and I raised him to be a devout Jewish carpenter. After his ministry began, I visited with him as often as I could while Joseph continued to meet the needs of his clients.

I was in Jerusalem for Passover when Jesus was arrested. He had warned me during one of his visits to Nazareth that it would happen, so it was no surprise. It was very difficult for me to hear people among the crowd around me shouting, "Crucify him!" I wanted to scream at them, but I could not.

When the soldiers drove nails into my son, it felt as though the nails were driven through my heart. My eyes were so flooded with tears, sometimes I could hardly see. One of the sons of Zebedee kept his arm around me, comforting me. My husband, Joseph, had died, and John, the man who stood with me, was part of my son's plans.

> *When Jesus saw his mother and the disciple whom he loved standing nearby, he said to his mother, "Woman, behold, your son!" Then he said to the disciple, "Behold, your mother!" And from that hour the disciple took her to his own home.*
> [John 19:26-27 (ESV)]

Both John and his older brother, James, were among "the twelve," the men closest to my son. Those two men were huge, barrel-chested men, who Jesus called "sons of thunder" because of their loud voices. Of the twelve, I think my son was closest to John, perhaps because he was the youngest.

God had blessed John with only fourteen years when he began following my son. As we stood there at the cross, John had just celebrated the seventeenth anniversary of his birth. I had already celebrated many more such anniversaries than he had.

After watching Joseph and his servants putting my son's body in the tomb, John took me to lodgings in the city with the families of the twelve. Throughout the Sabbath and after our first meal the first day following, the men continued to meet in an upper room.

John and the others were surprised and joyously delighted to see Jesus after he was resurrected. When it was time to move on, I packed John's belongings and mine. We thanked our hosts for their hospitality, and we set out for Capernaum. Although Joseph's family included many people, Jesus had put me in John's care, and I already knew the Zebedee family quite well. For well over a month, Jesus continued to appear from time to time in various places. I was not there when John and the others saw my son ascend into heaven, but my heart was full of him, and it always will be.

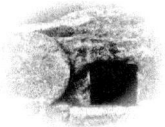

The Testimony of
John

John was youngest of the twelve apostles and outlived the rest of them.

Many people say I was closer to Jesus than his other friends. I suppose this was because of my being the youngest. I had just come of age when Jesus called my brother James and me to follow him. Our father, Zebedee, nodded his ascent as he continued our family's fishing work. James and I left our nets to follow Jesus.

I was sixteen three years later, when Jesus washed our feet on the night he was betrayed, the Passover meal seemed somehow different, and I sensed a crisis. The next day, as I stood near the foot of Jesus' cross with his mother, I sensed that the world had changed forever, but time would pass before I fully understood why. When Jesus said, *"Behold, your mother,"* I was more than willing to take the responsibility in the middle of our sadness.

My entire family is boisterous. We have always worked hard and played hard. We don't do anything timidly. When we're at a celebration, we're the loudest. That may be why Jesus called James and I "sons of thunder."

When I told Mary that Peter, myself, and some others had eaten broiled fish and bread with

Jesus one morning, she was happy for me. I was not surprised that she did not say she wished she had been there. That was the way she was, even until she went home to heaven. Whatever happened in her life, she accepted it as part of God's plan in God's world.

I told Mary what Jesus had said after we'd had breakfast. Peter had asked about me, wondering what was to happen to me as the youngest. My Lord's response was puzzling at the time for me.

> *Jesus answered, "If I want him to remain alive until I return, what is that to you? You must follow me."* [John 21:22 (NIV2011)]

It was because of that answer, there was a rumor that I would never die. That, of course, was absurd.

On the first day of the following week, I was mending a net, working by myself, and Jesus appeared and joined me as I worked. We talked like friends and coworkers, which is a fond memory for me. He knew I would take care of his mother until she left her physical body behind and put on her spiritual body. Jesus knew about my interest in Cappadocia, Galatia, and Asia. He did not tell me that he would see me again after I was exiled to Patmos.

I have written another letter to the disciples in Ephesus about exiled life here on this little island in the Aegean Sea. Each day I have tried to get exercise and explore the island. Recently on the Lord's day, I was in a cave up on a hill where I had gone the previous day. I heard a loud voice behind me, louder than anyone's voice in my family had ever been.

> *...which said: "Write on a scroll what you see and send it to the seven churches: to Ephesus, Smyrna, Pergamum, Thyatira, Sardis, Philadelphia and Laodicea." I turned around to see the voice that was speaking to me. And when I turned I saw seven golden lampstands, and among the lampstands was someone like a son of man, dressed in a robe reaching down to his feet and with a golden sash around his chest. The hair on his head was white like wool, as white as snow, and his eyes were like blazing fire. His feet were like bronze glowing in a furnace, and his voice was like the sound of rushing waters.*
> [Revelation 1:11-15 (NIV 2011)]

He took me on a sort of spiritual journey that lasted the rest of the day. I want others to know about that day and that vision, so I am writing a description of the vision. I'm sending it to a friend, along with this testimony.

I know that I will not remain here on Patmos much longer. It does not matter. This world is not my home. Having seen the vision that Jesus gave me, I know that I am simply passing through, on to eternity. My heart is always full.

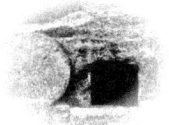

The Testimony of
Nicodemus

Nicodemus was a Pharisee who first encountered Jesus at the beginning of his ministry.

When Joseph retrieved the body of Jesus from His cross, I was with him, watching my friend and fellow Pharisee. I'd brought about a hundred pounds of myrrh and aloes to pack around the body, which Joseph's servants used. As a scribe, I knew the law much better than most, and the push to get rid of Jesus was enormous. Joseph and I were among the few dissenting votes on the Sanhedrin Council when it was determined that Jesus should be put to death.

We were both convinced that Jesus (Yeshua Bar Joseph) was the Messiah (Hebrew) or the Christ (Greek). We were the small minority on the council, and it was our secret. When I heard from friends in Emmaus that they had seen Jesus after his resurrection, I felt compelled to investigate.

I sent one of my servants to tell Joseph. He asked me to keep him informed, but that he could not join me in searching for Messiah. Despite his wealth and influence, Joseph and his family were being watched by others on the Sanhedrin Council because he had given up his tomb for Jesus.

I decided to go north by way of the Jordan river. By taking that route, there were fewer chances I would encounter anyone whom I knew. I just loaded a donkey with some of my older clothing, started north, and kept to myself. The first people I encountered who said they had seen him, I simply overheard as I was having an evening meal in Tiberias. I did not join the conversation. During the night, I prayed about what I had learned, and after resting for a day, I decided to continue going north.

The next day, I decided to walk closer to the Sea of Galilee because Jesus had taught along the shore so many times. I received no answers to my inquiries in Magdala, so I continued north to Capernaum. That little town was Jesus' base of operations for much of his three years of ministry. I remained there nearly a week, making quiet inquiries of the fishermen and of the innkeepers. I began to think that Jesus had gone home to heaven before I could see him.

On the Sabbath, I went into the synagogue. I knew Simon, the rabbi there, because of conversations we had over many years during the holy day celebrations. During Sukkot (Feast of the Tabernacles), I usually pitched a tent on Simon's roof. He took me aside in the evening and told me that several men had told him a rumor that Jesus might appear soon in Bethsaida. Rabbi Simon told me that if I wished to go there, that he would like to travel with me. I agreed.

The first day of the week, we arrived in Bethsaida in the evening, and we were able to secure lodging before sunset. As we shared barley bread, some vegetables and fruit, there was ample wine. There was also pickled fish, but both of us declined. Word had spread throughout the area that Jesus would supposedly appear soon, and the inn overflowed with patrons.

Two days later, while we were having a simple breakfast of barley bread and wine, a man came in and raised his voice to call out, "He's here!" He turned and left. Simon and I quickly went outside and began to follow a stream of men headed for the northern shore of the Sea of Galilee. As the water came into view for us, we could see Our Master moving about in a large crowd. There were hundreds of us.

> *For I delivered to you as of first importance what I also received: that Christ died for our sins in accordance with the Scriptures, that he was buried, that he was raised on the third day in accordance with the Scriptures, and that he appeared to Cephas, then to the twelve. Then he appeared to more than five hundred brothers at one time, most of whom are still alive, though some have fallen asleep.* [1 Corinthians 15:3-6 (ESV)]

Throughout the day, Jesus talked with us. He spoke about how we were to love one another as a community of faith. He also told us we were to spread the good news about his victory over death. He talked to us about how we were to lead others to follow him, and to build up the faith of those in the community. Building one another up in our faith was to include teaching one another how to multiply our numbers.

It was so very good to hear his voice again. Just before he vanished, he told us he was going to spend time with his brother, James, and with the remaining eleven of his inner circle.

After Simon and I spent another night at the inn, I walked with him back to Capernaum, I spent the night with his family, and then I continued south the next morning with a full heart.

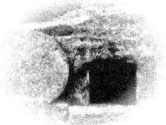

The Testimony of
James Ben Joseph

James was Jesus' brother through Joseph, the husband of Mary.

As I sat among hundreds of men near Bethsaida and listening to my brother, Jesus, I could not help but think about how much things had dramatically changed. In childhood, I had four brothers, including Jesus, Joseph, Simon, and Judas. We had five sisters, and we all played with each other when we were very young, but after we became of age, we seldom saw one another after our weddings except on Holy days. When we traveled as a family to Jerusalem for holy days such as Passover, I sometimes overheard our mother and father talk with Jesus about things I did not understand, but I did not ask about it.

After Jesus was baptized by our cousin, John, my brother became an itinerant rabbi. I heard some unbelievable things about him. I did not take the time to investigate what I was hearing because I was constantly busy, helping our father fulfill carpentry orders, and I had to tend to my wife and children's needs. I did not believe Jesus to be the Messiah.

When my brother was crucified, buried, and resurrected, everything changed. Three days after he rose from the dead, our mother sent word that her sons were to meet her in our father Joseph's house, which was then occupied by Simon and his family because our father had died. When we arrived, we saw that our mother Mary was accompanied by one of Jesus' closest friends, a young man named John.

After a meal of bread, fish, fruits, and wine, servants cleaned up around us. Our focus turned to Mary, our mother, but then Jesus appeared, saying, "You are here because I asked our mother to call for you. She was my voice because your father, Joseph, is with my Father in heaven." As I listened, I finally was certain Jesus was the Messiah.

Our conversation with my brother lasted through the night. None of us got any sleep, but we did not get tired. Most of the things he said were addressed to me because I was the oldest of the brothers on Earth. I learned during the night that, not only had I become the head of our family because Joseph was in heaven, I was to be the leader of the community of faith that was developing in Jerusalem.

My brother continued to appear. I had to be in Jerusalem for the celebration of Pentecost. It was nearly three weeks before Simon and I began listening to him again, there by the Sea of Galilee. I came to know that we would be guided for our journey, and I also knew that all we would need would be provided. I realized my heart had been mostly empty until I recognized my brother as Messiah. Then it became full.

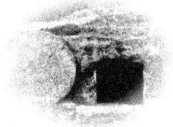

The Testimony of
Mary "the Magdalene"

Jesus cast out seven demons from Mary, and she traveled in the group that followed Him.

My husband was considerably older than I was, but I learned to love him. I bore seven children for him, and he was a good man. Shortly after I stopped being able to bear children, he died during grape harvest. Looking back, I think that's when demons filled me with rage. While our children and I were still grieving, and I was lashing out, my cousin in Nazareth invited me to visit. As a result, my youngest son, James, and two of my daughters were with me in the synagogue in Nazareth when Jesus stood up to read from the prophet Isaiah. Afterward, he put his hand on my shoulder while going past me, and looked at me. My rage and evil thoughts left me.

Afterward, I told James that my widowhood would have more meaning if I could serve Jesus. He and my cousin introduced me to three others that were serving while traveling with Jesus. From then on, I served while traveling with him for the next three years.

If you have never watched the execution of someone by crucifixion, I can only tell you that the experience is unforgettable. To watch a crucifixion is strangely fascinating, painful, and horrifying. Crowds are always there just for the spectacle. As I watched the nails being driven into my Lord, each blow with the hammer seemed to thrust the nail through all of me. My tears would not stop. When Jesus said, *"It is finished,"* and he surrendered his spirit, I died with him, or so it seemed. I was numb.

Several of us watched as two Pharisees retrieved the body and wrapped it in a shroud. We then followed them as they took him to a tomb. After putting the body inside, a stone was rolled in front of the entrance to seal it inside. We sat down and waited there until the sun set, and the light grew dim. Soldiers arrived to guard the tomb. We went and found shelter in Bethany.

During the Sabbath, we fasted and prayed. The other servants and I also developed a plan. Joseph had provided a shroud, and Nicodemus had supplied burial spices, but there had not been time to prepare our Lord for proper burial. We decided to return to the tomb the next day. Then we would give our Lord a proper burial. That was not to be.

When we got there, the stone had been rolled to one side from the entrance. Peter and John were walking away from the tomb, and two angels told us that he was not there – that he had risen from the dead. I thought I had drained all my tears on Friday, but I began weeping again – for joy – while the others were leaving.

I was curious. I went to the entrance and looked in.

> *And she saw two angels in white, sitting where the body of Jesus had lain, one at the head and one at the feet. They said to her, "Woman, why are you weeping?" She said to them, "They have taken away my Lord, and I do not know where they have laid him." Having said this, she turned around and saw Jesus standing, but she did not know that it was Jesus. Jesus said to her, "Woman, why are you weeping? Whom are you seeking?" Supposing him to be the gardener, she said to him, "Sir, if you have carried him away, tell me where you have laid him, and I will take him away." Jesus said to her, "Mary." She turned and said to him in Aramaic, "Rabboni!" (which means Teacher). Jesus said to her, "Do not cling to me, for I have not yet ascended to the Father; but go to my brothers and say to them, 'I am ascending to my Father and your Father, to my God and your God.'"* [John 20: 12-17 (ESV)]

I went and told the disciples.

When I learned that Jesus' mother was being cared for by the young John, I asked if I could travel with them to Capernaum. They agreed. I continued to travel with them for nearly six weeks, which meant I got to see my Lord again when they did.

Finally, shortly before Pentecost, they walked with me south to Magdala, and I was reunited with my family. One of my sons put on a feast of celebration, and we properly thanked

John and Jesus' mother. Our hearts would be forever full.

They went on their way.

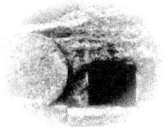

The Testimony of
"Mahdi"

"Mahdi" was a possessed man whose demons departed into a herd of pigs, and he became an evangelist in his town of Gerasa.

The people from my village and followers of Jesus know that my testimony is true. Others are at least skeptical. Originally, my ancient village was known as Garshu. When the Roman Empire expanded to include our village, the Romans Hellenized the Arabic name of our village and renamed it Gerasa. I don't remember my early childhood. My cousins have told me that when I witnessed my parents and brothers being killed by a Roman soldier, that I ran into the forest and disappeared. My cousins say they searched for me, but they did not see me for more than a month. By then I was out of control.

> *He lived among the tombs. And no one could bind him anymore, not even with a chain, for he had often been bound with shackles and chains, but he wrenched the chains apart, and he broke the shackles in pieces. No one had the strength to subdue him. Night and day among the tombs and on the mountains, he was always crying out and cutting himself with stones.*
> [Mark 5:3-5 (ESV)]

After Jesus healed me, I learned that I had been known as the Gerasene demoniac.

I only remember very small portions of the time when I grew stronger and stronger. Then, one day, I saw a man getting out of a boat. I ran towards him and collapsed at his feet as I heard him saying, "Come out of the man you unclean spirit." [Mark 5:8b (ESV)]

I heard my voice shouting at him.

> *"What have you to do with me, Jesus, Son of the Most High God? I adjure you by God, do not torment me."*
> [Mark 5:7b (ESV)]

I felt lost, as though I was listening to a conversation, but I did not know what I was saying.

> *And Jesus asked him, "What is your name?" He replied, "My name is Legion, for we are many." And he begged him earnestly not to send them out of the country. Now a great herd of pigs was feeding there on the hillside, and they begged him, saying, "Send us to the pigs; let us enter them." So he gave them permission. And the unclean spirits came out and entered the pigs; and the herd, numbering about two thousand, rushed down the steep bank into the sea and drowned in the sea.* [Mark 5:9-13 (ESV)]

As those who were herding the pigs ran for my village, Jesus spoke to me quietly, and two of his followers gave me clothing I could wear. I felt free and more alive than I had ever been. Oh, how I loved talking with Jesus!

The herdsmen returned from the village, bringing others. I apologized to them for all the damage I had done. As we talked, they began to fear Jesus, and they quite respectfully asked him to leave the area. Jesus understood their fear, and he agreed. I wanted to go with him as one of his followers, but he told me to stay in my beloved town. He wanted me to tell everyone I met that the kingdom of God is at hand, and that they should repent and embrace this good news. Reluctantly, I agreed.

Three years passed. I married, and my wife and I had two sons and a daughter. I learned to read and immersed myself in the scriptures. With God's help, I became a rabbi. After his resurrection, I was among the crowd of men near Bethsaida when Jesus appeared there, he spoke to me and encouraged me.

From that day on, the good news I had been sharing became great news. I have endeavored to fill the hearts of others with Jesus, out of my own overflowing heart.

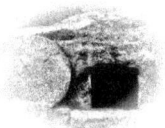

The Testimony of
Joseph

> Joseph was a Pharisee on the ruling council
> who buried the body of Jesus in his own tomb.

Although I have the same name as the earthly
father of Jesus, I know nothing about carpentry,
and I live far from Nazareth. As I grew up in
Arimathea, I had an uncle who was a Rabbi, and
he taught me to read. He taught me using
scriptures, which began on the fourth anniversary
of my birth. At first, I could not actually read, so
I memorized what Uncle Simon read to me. By the
time I came of age, I had memorized the Torah –
the Jewish books of the law –, and I had half
completed memorizing the writings.

My first wife brought me seven children
before she died in childbirth. I grieved for two
months, and then I married another virgin, who
gave me nine more children. I have always been a
good businessman, and God has blessed me in
many ways. By the time I was thirty, my success
and wealth were established and known. I became
part of the Sanhedrin.

Nicodemus was my best friend, and he still is.
When Jesus was baptized, he told me what
happened. From then on, when Jesus would come
to Jerusalem for the holy days, Nicodemus and I

would do our best to listen to him at every opportunity.

My friend and I voted against arranging the execution of Jesus, but Joseph Caiaphas got his way. He was powerful in part because he was the son-in-law of Annas Ben Seth. When Jesus entered Jerusalem on a donkey for that last Passover of his life on Earth, as I looked at him I knew in my heart that he was the Messiah. I was more than willing to give him my tomb after he was executed.

As we buried him, I heard something strange from one of my friends nearby who accompanied Nicodemus and me. It was about what happened when Jesus gave up his spirit.

> *And behold, the curtain of the temple was torn in two, from top to bottom. And the earth shook, and the rocks were split. The tombs also were opened. And many bodies of the saints who had fallen asleep were raised, and coming out of the tombs after his resurrection, they went into the holy city and appeared to many.* [Matthew 27:51-53 (ESV)]

Deep within me, I knew that Jesus' body would only be there in my tomb temporarily, and the tomb would still be the place of my burial. I hoped to see some of those who had risen from their tombs.

By handling a dead body and placing the body of Jesus into my tomb, several things happened. I became ceremonially unclean, so I could not partake of Passover with my family. What I had done became known, and several members of the Sanhedrin began to watch me closely. I had to be very careful with how I explained my reason for letting Jesus be buried in my tomb. I felt it would be unwise for me to join Nicodemus with others up north in Bethsaida, though I wanted to be there. I wanted to see the Messiah once again alive, but it was inadvisable.

For the safety of myself, my family, and my servants, I waited a full year before I sent word to James Ben Joseph, Jesus' brother. He said he was glad to hear from me, and he invited me to join him with other believers on the first day of each week for worship. It has been such a blessing to worship with others whose hearts are also full of Jesus.

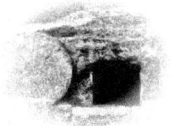

The Testimony of
"Jocasta"

"Jocasta" was not a Jew, but she startled Jesus with her profound faith, and he healed her daughter.

No one in Galilee knew my name until after Jesus' resurrection. I am not a Jew by birth. I am a Phoenician, and when I first met Jesus, I was from Tyre, in Syria. To this day, most people simply refer to me as the Syrophoenician woman.

When my oldest daughter was eight years of age, she became very sick. I cared for her as best I could, but my instinct as a mother told me that she was dying. A neighbor had a Jewish servant, who brought us some vegetable stew with pleasant spices for my daughter. My daughter refused it. The servant, an old man named Samuel, told me about a man named Jesus, who was healing people in the Galilee area.

My husband was away at war, so I left my daughter in the care of the neighbor and went to look for Jesus, who I was told was staying nearby. When I found him, I fell at his feet. I told him that my daughter was possessed by a demon, and I begged him to come and cast it out to heal my daughter. His initial response was not surprising. You see, in his eyes I was a Gentile, and Jews don't usually associate with Gentiles. I was determined, however.

> *And he said to her, "Let the children be fed*
> *first, for it is not right to take the children's*
> *bread and throw it to the dogs." But she*
> *answered him, "Yes, Lord; yet even the dogs*
> *under the table eat the children's crumbs."*
> [Mark 7:27-28 (ESV)]

That just boldly burst out of me! It was all I could
think of to say, but I was determined to have him
come and heal my daughter – after all, mothers
will be mothers!

As I looked into Jesus' face, I saw a look of
surprise. He gave me an unexpected response. I
will not forget what he said as long as I live. He
said to me,

> *"For this statement, you may go your way;*
> *the demon has left your daughter."*
> [Mark 7:29b (ESV)]

He did not even have to see my daughter! I was
stunned. When I got home, my daughter greeted
me at our doorway. I immediately went to my
neighbor's home and told the Jewish servant. He
fell upon his knees and praised God.

A week later, I learned that my husband had
been killed during a battle. By the time I heard
about it, he had already been buried near the
battlefield. I felt an emptiness, but he had often
been away at war, so there had been little love.
Our neighbors gathered around my daughter and
me as we grieved. As we ate and remembered my
husband, his brother asked me what I would now
do, since I was still of child-bearing age. It was
kind of him to ask, but deep within me, I knew I
had another option.

Seeing my neighbor's servant nearby, I approached Samuel. "Do you know of a Jewish man who would receive the daughter of a Gentile as his bride?" I asked him.

He nodded. "I have a brother named Bartholomew, who lives in Cana. The town is also known as Kafr Kanna, in Galilee. He lost his wife in childbirth three months ago. Shall I tell him about you?"

"Yes, if you will please."

That was my second beginning. Our marriage celebration was not at all like the one for my first marriage. I have become a Jew, and Bartholomew is a wonderful husband. He has many olive trees, and we earn a good living from the olive crops. He had previously met Jesus, before I did, at a wedding in his town of Cana. Both of us were always hungry of any news about Jesus.

Two years later, we heard that Jesus had been executed, but that He had risen from the dead. Bartholomew rushed with my daughter, our two sons, and I to Nazareth when we heard that Jesus had appeared there. We wanted to see him again because we assumed he would ascend to heaven soon. About twenty of us crowded into that home in Nazareth. Jesus spoke to each of us by name. I did not know that he knew my name, but he called me Jocasta, and he smiled at me.

My heart is forever full.

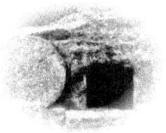

The Testimony of
Andrew

Andrew was the first man Jesus called to follow him, and Andrew previously was a disciple of John the Baptist.

I am a few years older than John, son of Zebedee. Shortly after I came of age, I became a disciple of John the Baptist. The man fascinated me, living the ascetic life and preaching a baptism for repentance. I really liked him. After he baptized Jesus one day, John told us more about him. Two of us decided that we would start following Jesus, and I went and told my brother, Simon. On impulse, he decided to join us for a while, to see what we could learn. We continued with our fishing business in Bethsaida, but we went to listen to Jesus near Capernaum when we could.

One evening we were repairing our nets when Jesus came and called us.

> *"Come, follow me," Jesus said, "and I will send you out to fish for people."*
> [Matthew 4:19 (NIV2011)]

Our lives have never been the same since then.

For the next three years, Simon and I, along with ten others, went with Jesus wherever he went except when he would withdraw to pray. When Jesus walked on the stormy Sea of Galilee, and when my brother saw that it was Jesus, Peter impulsively asked Jesus if he could join him out on the water. The rest of us stayed fearfully in the boat. I was not as brave or brash as my brother.

I never asked Jesus why he invited me to be part of his inner circle of friends. I'm not as strong as my brother. I'm not as smart as Judas was. I work hard and play hard, and I worship every day. I like to think of myself as a good father, but of course, no one is truly good except our heavenly Father.

> *Jesus said to him, "Why do you call me good?*
> *No one is good but God alone.*
> [Luke 18:19 (NRSV)]

That first evening after Jesus rose from the dead, Thomas was with his family, and Judas had hanged himself. The remaining ten of us were eating in the same room where we had celebrated Passover with the Master the previous week. When Jesus appeared at the table with us, I nearly dropped the chalice of wine I was holding.

Jesus showed us his wounds in his hands, his side, and his feet. Our somber meal suddenly became a meal of rejoicing. He told us that he was going to be around for a few weeks, and we were to go to Galilee, where he would spend more time with us. After each of us embraced him, he was gone again.

After he left, we decided to leave together the next day for Galilee. We could not sleep immediately, however. We reminded each other of things he had told us a few weeks earlier.

My command is this: Love each other as I have loved you. Greater love has no one than this: to lay down one's life for one's friends. You are my friends if you do what I command. I no longer call you servants, because a servant does not know his master's business. Instead, I have called you friends, for everything that I learned from my Father I have made known to you. You did not choose me, but I chose you and appointed you so that you might go and bear fruit—fruit that will last—and so that whatever you ask in my name the Father will give you. This is my command: Love each other.

[John 15:12-17 (NIV2011)]

We knew that "Love each other" did not refer to physical attraction. We knew he did not mean merely brother love. We also knew Jesus did not refer to love like that of a parent for a child. Invariably, Jesus talked about unconditional, unlimited, and selfless love. Such love comes from God and flows through us.

As we went north, we told everyone we encountered that Jesus is alive. Since Simon and I had both family and business in Bethsaida, we invited the others to go with us there. We saw Jesus several times before he ascended. Even after Jesus returned to heaven, our hearts remained full.

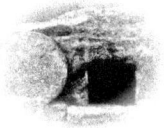

The Testimony of
"Phoebe"

"Phoebe" was a woman with a bad reputation
that washed Jesus' feet with her tears of
remorse and repentance.

I don't have much to say, but I think you
may find it important. No one knew my name,
though I'm sure Jesus knew. After he became well
known, he and his closest followers were invited to
an evening meal at the home of a Pharisee named
Simon. I was not invited, of course, but I wanted
Jesus to know I was sorry about my life, and I
loved him.

> *A woman in that town who lived a sinful life*
> *learned that Jesus was eating at the*
> *Pharisee's house, so she came there with an*
> *alabaster jar of perfume. As she stood behind*
> *him at his feet weeping, she began to wet his*
> *feet with her tears. Then she wiped them with*
> *her hair, kissed them and poured perfume on*
> *them.* [Luke 7:37-38 (NIV 2011)]

I have no doubt that Simon knew my bad
reputation in our town. For a fee, I made myself
available to men for their needs. Simon was
probably tempted to have his servants throw me
out, but he didn't because of Jesus. I think that
Jesus knew what Simon was thinking because he
told the Pharisee he wanted to tell him something.

Simon told him he would listen, so Jesus responded, asking him about forgiveness and love. Simon said that those who are forgiven more are loved more, and Jesus agreed. Jesus did not stop there, however.

> *Then he turned toward the woman and said to Simon, "Do you see this woman? I came into your house. You did not give me any water for my feet, but she wet my feet with her tears and wiped them with her hair. You did not give me a kiss, but this woman, from the time I entered, has not stopped kissing my feet. You did not put oil on my head, but she has poured perfume on my feet. Therefore, I tell you, her many sins have been forgiven— as her great love has shown. But whoever has been forgiven little loves little."*
> [Luke 7:44-47 (NIV2011)]

Jesus then told me my sins were forgiven. When I left, I knew I had to change. My father had died, so I went to my oldest brother, told him I had repented, and I wanted him to secure a husband for me.

After Jesus rose from the dead, my husband and I were in Cana when Jesus appeared there. He smiled and greeted me by name, and my heart has been overflowing for him ever since.

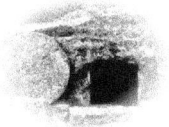

The Testimony of
Thomas

"Doubting" Thomas was a bold and brave man
who was one of the twelve apostles.

I have no problem admitting my failure. The first time Jesus appeared to our circle of his closest friends after his crucifixion, I was not there. I was with my family, but it does not matter why. When the others told me that Jesus was alive, I simply could not believe it. It wasn't that I did not trust them. We were willing to trust one another with our lives. When I heard it, it just seemed too incredible to believe. I said, *"Unless I see the nail marks in his hands and put my finger where the nails were, and put my hand into his side, I will not believe."* [John 20:25b (NIV2011)] I had seen many miracles – even frightening miracles – but that my Lord was alive seemed beyond belief.

My disbelief only lasted a week. Jesus was not done with me, but I did not know it at the time.

> *A week later, his disciples were in the house again, and Thomas was with them. Though the doors were locked, Jesus came and stood among them and said, "Peace be with you!" Then he said to Thomas, "Put your finger here; see my hands. Reach out your hand and put it into my side. Stop doubting and believe."* [John 20:26-27 (NIV2011)]

He then taught us something crucially important, which I passed on for the rest of my days on Earth. Jesus said to me, *"Have you believed because you have seen me? Blessed are those who have not seen and yet have believed."* [John 20:29 (ESV)]

Just before he ascended into heaven a few weeks later, Jesus commissioned us to go beyond our boundaries and spread the good news. For some reason, when Jesus said that, I knew that I would be traveling across some great distances, even beyond the Roman Empire. As I realized that, I had no fear, and I have never again had a sense of doubt. Memories of my beloved Jesus always have filled my heart.

As I watched his ascension into heaven, I was not sad. In fact, I was filled with joy and a sense of purpose. The next day I purchased a camel and provisions for my travels. Traveling north through Syria, I was able to baptize a number of people in Tyre and other towns. I lingered in Dura Europos for over a year. Then I urged some of them to go to Cana and get more instruction. I knew there were believers there. The Holy Spirit urged me to travel further north.

When I arrived in Yerevan in Armenia, I encountered Bartholomew and Thaddeus, who I had not seen since Jesus ascended. They had been there nearly a year, and they had already baptized more than fifty believers. Many times, over the following month, I witnessed to my experiences with Jesus, and I prophesied what the Holy Spirit gave me to say. I told them that if Bartholomew and Thaddeus continued their work there, that eventually the entire region would surrender to Jesus.

One evening, while we were breaking bread together, a believer named Abaven had the Holy Spirit come upon him. He told me that the Lord wanted me to journey eastward, to a city named Muziris. [It is a town in northern India.] I am sending this testimony to James in Jerusalem. I hope that it reaches him. I know his heart is full of his brother, and Jesus continues to fill my heart as well.

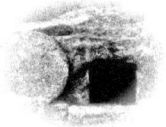

The Testimony of
"Photini"

"Photini" met Jesus by a well at the Samaritan city of Sychar and became a disciple.

Most people in Samaria get married. Women often get married while in their teens, and men sometimes wait until they are in their mid-to-late twenties. Death frequently comes suddenly. Men die in battle, and women die in childbirth. Many of us are widowed and remarried more than once. Most of us get married without a dowry or a contract. When two people establish a home together, that tells the community they are married. I have had more than one husband. Death is all too common. Each of my husbands has encouraged me to seek after God with them.

One day, I was helping a neighbor in Sychar do her laundry and care for her children. I asked for her advice because there was a widower who wanted to marry me. While we talked, we needed more water, so I went to the well. As I drew the water up from the well, some men came up the road. Most of them continued into town, but one of them lingered at the well. I could tell he was Jewish, but I had never seen him before. He asked me to give him a drink, and I asked him how it was that a Jew would ask a Samaritan woman for a drink. His answer caught me off guard.

> *"If you knew the gift of God, and who it is*
> *that is saying to you, 'Give me a drink,' you*
> *would have asked him, and he would have*
> *given you living water."* [John 4:10 (ESV)]

I pointed out that the well was deep, and that he
had nothing with which to draw water. I
expressed wonder to him, asking if he was greater
than our father Jacob, who gave us the well.
Again, he surprised me with his answer.

> *Jesus said to her, "Everyone who drinks of*
> *this water will be thirsty again, but whoever*
> *drinks of the water that I will give him will*
> *never be thirsty again. The water that I will*
> *give him will become in him a spring of water*
> *welling up to eternal life."*
> [John 4:13-14 (ESV)]

When I asked him for some of the living water, he
told me to call my husband. When I told him I
had no husband, he proceeded to tell me more
about myself than I had ever told anyone. I knew
then he was a prophet. He talked with me about
many things. After learning his name was Jesus, I
went back into Sychar. I told them what he had
said. We all wondered if he could be a prophet, or
perhaps the Messiah.

Many people left what they were doing to
come to the well and see Jesus. That was a new
beginning for many of us in Sychar. Jesus and his
friends stayed with us for two days. After he left,
many of us began worshiping God in a new way
with new life. As I look back, I think Jesus chose
me to spread the good news to those I knew in

Samaria. With that visit, a community of believers was established outside of Judaism.

I did not see Jesus again for many months. When travelers brought word to us that Jesus had been crucified, we wept. Less than a week later, other travelers told us that he was alive again and was appearing in Galilee, north of Tabor. My then husband was a man who had a large vineyard. We left instructions with our servants, and we journeyed north, hoping to see Jesus again.

About a week later, my husband and I were traveling between Tiberias and Magdala. Another man began walking with us. He joined in our conversation, asking about our discussion. My husband said, "We are Samaritans. We are part of a religious community that believes that a man named Jesus is the Jewish Messiah. After he was crucified, we heard that he is alive again. We are traveling north to try to see him if we can."

"That is interesting." He said that he was a Jew, and that he knew of these things. As we walked towards the Sea of Galilee, we talked about the many prophecies concerning the Messiah. When we got to the Sea, we stepped into the water with cups to get a drink. As we drank together, we looked at one another's faces directly for the first time. It was Jesus! He smiled and spoke to us by name for a few moments. Then he vanished.

When my husband and I returned to Sychar, we told other believers that we had seen him. My husband composed a letter and sent it to the apostles in Jerusalem. They sent some believers to

us, and we established a church community in
Sychar. Our hearts are always compassionate and
full of love. We have Jesus in our hearts as our
Savior, best friend, and constant companion.

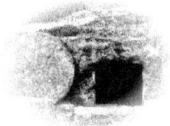

The Testimony of
Simon / Peter

Peter was a brash and enthusiastic apostle among the twelve, whom Roman Catholics consider to be the first pope.

I have testified countless times about Jesus as I have moved about and shared the good news. Sometimes I have been brief, and sometimes I've spoken for hours. This time I shall speak only about the time between his resurrection and his ascension.

First, however, I must respond to questions that have been asked about Judas. I was with Judas nearly every day for three years. I thought I knew him, and I considered him a close friend. I cannot erase from my mind any instance in which he was beside me or near me when Jesus performed one of his signs.

When we were battling a storm together on the Sea of Galilee, and while Jesus was asleep, we were all frightened. When we awakened him, the fear of all twelve of us was turned towards awe.

> *And they went and woke him, saying, "Master, Master, we are perishing!" And he awoke and rebuked the wind and the raging waves, and they ceased, and there was a calm.*
> [Luke 8:24 (ESV)]

Fear of the storm became amazed fear of our
Lord's awesome power. Judas shared in all our
experiences.

When we were battling another storm,
suddenly the twelve of us, including Judas, saw
Jesus walking towards us on the water.

> *But when the disciples saw him walking on
> the sea, they were terrified, and said, "It is a
> ghost!" and they cried out in fear. But
> immediately Jesus spoke to them, saying,
> "Take heart; it is I. Do not be afraid." And
> Peter answered him, "Lord, if it is you,
> command me to come to you on the water."
> He said, "Come." So Peter got out of the boat
> and walked on the water and came to Jesus.
> But when he saw the wind, he was afraid,
> and beginning to sink he cried out, "Lord,
> save me." Jesus immediately reached out his
> hand and took hold of him, saying to him, "O
> you of little faith, why did you doubt?"*
> [Matthew 14:26-31 (ESV)]

Although Judas stayed in the boat with the other
ten, the twelve of us experienced all of it as close-
knit brothers. We were all close.

Then Judas betrayed our master. My heart
broke when that happened, and I was furious. I
think I must have hated Judas there in the garden
of Gethsemane. Yes, he later repented and killed
himself. In my memories of Judas, my feelings are
mixed, even if it is true that he used some of the
money from our common purse for himself. I am
truly sorry that Judas never got to see Jesus risen
from the dead.

As joyous as I felt when I saw Jesus alive on the first day of the week after his crucifixion, and even though I saw him other times after his resurrection, my fondest memory of my Master is centered a few days later, when six of my brothers and I went fishing. We fished from sundown to sunrise but caught nothing all night.

In the pre-dawn light, we dimly saw a man on the shore in the shadows of the hills.

> *Jesus said to them, "Children, do you have any fish?" They answered him, "No." He said to them, "Cast the net on the right side of the boat, and you will find some." So they cast it, and now they were not able to haul it in, because of the quantity of fish. That disciple whom Jesus loved therefore said to Peter, "It is the Lord!" When Simon Peter heard that it was the Lord, he put on his outer garment, for he was stripped for work, and threw himself into the sea.*
> [John 21:5-7 (ESV)]

I was excited, yet I wondered when I saw that he already had a charcoal fire there with fish and bread. He told us to bring some of the 153 fish we had caught to the fire. We ate breakfast together and enjoyed each other's company.

After breakfast, Jesus began talking with me.

> *When they had finished breakfast, Jesus said to Simon Peter, "Simon, son of John, do you love me more than these?" He said to him, "Yes, Lord; you know that I love you." He said to him, "Feed my lambs." He said to him a second time, "Simon, son of John, do you love me?" He said to him, "Yes, Lord; you know that I love*

you." He said to him, "Tend my sheep." He said to him the third time, "Simon, son of John, do you love me?" Peter was grieved because he said to him the third time, "Do you love me?" and he said to him, "Lord, you know everything; you know that I love you." Jesus said to him, "Feed my sheep. Truly, truly, I say to you, when you were young, you used to dress yourself and walk wherever you wanted, but when you are old, you will stretch out your hands, and another will dress you and carry you where you do not want to go." (This he said to show by what kind of death he was to glorify God.) And after saying this he said to him, "Follow me."

[John 21:15-19 (ESV)]

The first time, with his response I knew he forgave me for denying I knew him that night in which he was betrayed by Judas. The second time, was his way of telling me that he still expected a great deal of me. That encouraged and strengthened me in many ways I can't put into words.

As our conversation concluded, I felt closer to Jesus than I ever had on any occasion, including when he invited me to walk on water with him. I know there are others just as blessed as I am. Why? Because I know people who believe in him, just as I do, yet they never saw him in person.

I am encouraged by all those faithful followers who serve him tirelessly even though they won't meet him face to face until he welcomes them into heaven. Yes, my heart is full of Jesus, but my heart is also full for all of those who serve him with me.

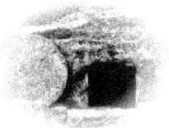

The Testimony of
Matthias

> The twelve apostles wanted someone to replace Judas, and prayer and prophesy helped them choose Matthias.

Who am I? Again, I ask, who am I? If it were not for Jesus and his resurrection, I would not be anyone. I am just like everyone who has Jesus dwelling in their heart. My only distinction is simply based upon one brief event. After Jesus ascended, and shortly before Pentecost, the inner circle of Jesus' followers wanted to replace Judas. It had to be someone who, like them, had seen Jesus after he had risen from the dead. Peter said that it had to be someone who had been with the twelve from the beginning. Since everyone is a sinner, casting lots to invite God to choose was the only procedure that made sense. They prayed.

> *And they prayed and said, "You, Lord, who know the hearts of all, show which one of these two you have chosen to take the place in this ministry and apostleship from which Judas turned aside to go to his own place."*
> [Acts 1:24-25 (ESV)]

There were about one hundred twenty witnesses to the resurrection in Jerusalem at the time. They first narrowed it down to two people. I was one of them. The other man was named Joseph, who was also known either as Barsabbas or as Justus. When they cast lots, God told them through the lots it was to be me.

I saw Jesus several times during those five weeks and five days after he was resurrected. I then made my way to Cappadocia and spent time on the coasts of the Caspian Sea. My wife and I eventually set up a house church near Issus, one of the ports on that body of water. The Lord used me to lead many people to a saving relationship with Jesus. Our five sons and four daughters found fulfillment in joining their parents in doing what so many of Jesus' closest friends did. God gave us success at both catching and preserving fish, and at fishing for people that they may be saved for eternity,

My wife laughed when we heard a rumor that I had died in Aethiopia. That was one of several rumors about us that we heard while living near Issus. Actually, we left our children there and returned to Jerusalem to meet with believers there. We stayed several years, and since my wife has died since then, I have decided to spend the rest of my days in the Holy City with a full heart. Then I shall go home and join my wife.

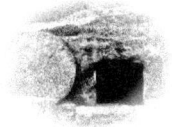

The Testimony of
"Filippos"

"Filippos" was partially paralyzed when his
friends took him to Jesus for healing.

I must give my testimony because I have such
good friends. It is because of them that I met
Jesus. I awakened one morning with my right side
totally useless. That part of me would not
function, and I could feel nothing there. Doctors
tried everything from herbs to bleeds, but there
was no result. It was very hard to eat and drink,
even my best wines from my vineyards.

My friends heard about a rabbi named Jesus,
who was not very far away. My friends carried me
for more than two hours until they reached the
crowd. They could not get through, and they
needed to get me into the house. My friends
decided to let me down through the roof.

I do not know about other parts of the Roman
Empire, but in Galilee the roof is important to our
living. It is always flat. A roof is like a second
room, but outside. The law of Moses says it must
have guard rails to protect people from falling.

My friends made an opening in the roof
between the timbers, and they let me down
through it.

When they could not find a way to do this
because of the crowd, they went up on the roof

> *and lowered him on his mat through the tiles into*
> *the middle of the crowd, right in front of Jesus.*
> *When Jesus saw their faith, he said, "Friend,*
> *your sins are forgiven."*
> [Luke 5:19-20 (NIV2011)]

I had never heard such a thing spoken by a Rabbi. I
was dumbfounded! Besides, my friends brought me
to him for healing, not to be forgiven.

Then I looked around, and I recognized some
Pharisees and scribes that I had seen at the temple
when I was there for holy days, before I got sick.
They were murmuring among themselves, and
obviously they were upset. I looked at Jesus' face,
and I could tell he understood. He spoke to them.

> *Jesus knew what they were thinking and asked,*
> *"Why are you thinking these things in your*
> *hearts? Which is easier: to say, 'Your sins are*
> *forgiven,' or to say, 'Get up and walk'? But I*
> *want you to know that the Son of Man has*
> *authority on earth to forgive sins." So he said*
> *to the paralyzed man, "I tell you, get up, take*
> *your mat and go home."*
> [Luke 5:22-24 (NIV2011)]

I felt warm all over. I felt like I was full of
energy and strong. I sat up, and I felt wonderful.
He told me to pick up my mat and go home, so I
did, praising God as I went. I hope I thanked him!
I think I did.

After he was resurrected, I was in a crowd
when he appeared on the north shore of the Sea of
Galilee. I think he saw me and recognized me. I
hope so. My heart felt full as I walked out,
carrying my mat. My heart still feels full.

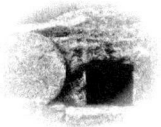

An Epilogue by
Saul/Paul

> Paul met Jesus on the road to Damascus as a
> blinding light from the sky, sometime later,
> after the ascension.

Jesus and I were born about the same time. I
did not know him in the flesh, either prior to his
crucifixion or during the days between his
resurrection and ascension. As I said to the church
in Corinth,

> *Last of all, as to one untimely born, he appeared*
> *also to me. For I am the least of the apostles,*
> *unworthy to be called an apostle, because I*
> *persecuted the church of God.*
> [1 Corinthians 15:8-9 (ESV)]

After so many others had seen him after his
resurrection, and after he ascended, some time
passed before he appeared to me. As a zealous
rabbi, I had authority from the Sanhedrin to
arrest the followers of Jesus.

> *But Saul, still breathing threats and murder*
> *against the disciples of the Lord, went to the high*
> *priest and asked him for letters to the synagogues*
> *at Damascus, so that if he found any belonging*
> *to the Way, men or women, he might bring them*
> *bound to Jerusalem. Now as he went on his way,*
> *he approached Damascus, and suddenly a light*
> *from heaven shone around him. And falling to*
> *the ground he heard a voice saying to him,*

"Saul, Saul, why are you persecuting me?" And he said, "Who are you, Lord?" And he said, "I am Jesus, whom you are persecuting. But rise and enter the city, and you will be told what you are to do." The men who were traveling with him stood speechless, hearing the voice but seeing no one.[Acts 9:1-7 (ESV)]

Up until that time, I was spiritually blind. After Jesus spoke to me, I was a new man, with an amazing spiritual awareness. At the same time, I was physically blind. I continued to Damascus, where Jesus had arranged for a man named Ananias to heal me. It took some time to convince other believers that I was a changed man, and that Jesus had changed me.

Since then, I have met most of his inner circle of friends in my visits to Jerusalem. The Holy Spirit has led me to many communities of Rome's empire. Soon I will go to Rome, where I am to appear before Caesar.

I have met many people who saw the risen Messiah. My calling is to introduce Jesus to those who did not know him. I am under obligation to everyone – to Greeks, barbarians, men, women, slaves or free. The good news is the power of God to save everyone.

No matter where I go, nothing and no one can separate me from the love of Christ.

For I am sure that neither death nor life, nor angels nor rulers, nor things present nor things to come, nor powers, nor height nor depth, nor anything else in all creation, will be able to separate us from the love of God in Christ Jesus our Lord.

[Romans 8:38-39 (ESV)]

I have seen that anyone who has Jesus filling their heart has some of his attributes. Each of us who follows him is a new creation. Having a part of Jesus at work in us is his gift to us. Though I have a thorn in my flesh, Jesus has given me the gifts I need to do whatever he calls me to do. His grace is sufficient.

Believers have told me many times, once they invite Jesus into their hearts, they have a new sense of purpose and direction. I know that has been true for me. When I was persecuting Christians, I was driven by rage, and that rage consumed much of my life. Once Jesus called me, I had no time for rage. My heart since then has been full.

Other books by James J. Stewart at Amazon.com:

Christian Fiction

An Extensive Life
[The life story of a Christian man more than four hundred years old.]

A Nation Transformed
[In 2042, God uses miracles to transform the USA.

Casting Lots
[A young adults Christian romance and adventure set in the near future]

Prayer Warriors
[Urban adventures in a near-future continuation of *Casting Lots*]

Soul Mates
[Another Christian Romance in the same setting as *Tom's Town*]

The Camera Doctors
[Two people meet on top of a famous mountain, and romance ensues.]

The Gaardian Saga
[Christian science fiction fantasy with multiple romances]

This World Is Not My Home
[A couple together since high school separates to find great loves with others.]

Tom's Town
[Small town life and Christian romance in California's Sierra Foothills]

Christian Poetry and Inspiration

Faith and Yosemite
[Christian poetry with pictures of Yosemite]

Faith Fuel
[Meditations on the Christian faith and life]

Lasting Love
[Short Biographical Sketches]

Living for Jesus
[Bible Study Guide for Couples and Small Groups]

Seed Thoughts for Christian Prayer and Meditation
[Workbook]

Single Sentence Sermons
[Workbook for growing faith]

Walking in Faith
[Much of the same poetry as *Faith and Yosemite* but without pictures]